THE STORIES OF HANS·ANDERSEN

Retold by

ROBERT MATHIAS

Illustrated by

ROBIN LAWRIE

Silver Burdett Company
Morristown, New Jersey

First published 1985 by
Hamlyn Publishing
A division of The Hamlyn Publishing Group Limited.,
Bridge House, London Road, Twickenham, Middlesex, England.

Adapted and published
in the United States in 1985 by
Silver Burdett Company
Morristown, New Jersey

Library of Congress Cataloging in Publication Data

Mathias, Robert.
   The stories of Hans Andersen.

   Summary: Retells six well-known fairy tales by the
Danish author including "The Emperor's New Clothes"
and "The Little Mermaid."
   1. Fairy tales—Denmark.   2. Children's stories,
Danish—Translations into English.   3. Children's
stories, English—Translations from Danish.   [1. Fairy
tales.   2. Short stories]   I. Andersen, H. C. (Hans
Christian), 1805–1875.   II. Lawrie, Robin, ill
III. Title.
PZ8.M44873St 1985   [E]   85-61399
ISBN 0-382-09153-1
Printed in Italy

Contents

The Snow Queen

LONG AGO AT THE BEGINNING OF TIME the devil sat in his workshop and made an evil mirror. It reflected the beauty of the earth but when the devil looked into it all beauty vanished and turned into loathsome ugliness. The fresh-scented forests of pines became withered, slime-covered swamps; flowers turned black, crumpled up and died and butterflies lost their color and became spiky, poisonous creatures. But worst of all was what the mirror did to a human face: no matter how beautiful, it was twisted and distorted into a hideous, misshapen mask.

The devil was pleased – the mirror would help his evil work. He took up the thigh-bone of a wolf and brought it down violently onto the mirror. It smashed into a million fragments and instantly a howl of wind screamed into the workshop. The wind whisked the splinters into the air and sent them spinning around the devil's head and he laughed out loud. The glass splinters tumbled and twisted and the devil laughed even louder. The louder he laughed the more the wind swirled the deadly slivers about his head. Soon he was laughing so loudly that the broken fragments were scattered like an evil whirlwind all around the world. Tiny pieces were blown into every nook and cranny, in all directions. They would do the devil's work – and he laughed even louder at the thought of the sorrow they would bring.

*　　　*　　　*

In the great city of Copenhagen lived a little girl called Gerda. She was very poor, and apart from the love of her parents, had nothing to brighten her life except the friendship of her neighbor, Kai. His house was right next door to hers and they loved each other like brother and sister. They were never happier than when they were together.

The two families lived high up in the attics right under the roofs of the houses. These were so close that apart from a thin strip of sky, they

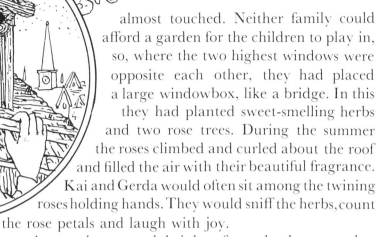

almost touched. Neither family could afford a garden for the children to play in, so, where the two highest windows were opposite each other, they had placed a large windowbox, like a bridge. In this they had planted sweet-smelling herbs and two rose trees. During the summer the roses climbed and curled about the roof and filled the air with their beautiful fragrance. Kai and Gerda would often sit among the twining roses holding hands. They would sniff the herbs, count the rose petals and laugh with joy.

The days were long and warm and their love for each other grew, day by day, just like the climbing roses.

When Winter came and set his hand over the city, the children could no longer play in their garden; all the windows were bolted tight against the chill winds that beat upon them. The children would then take a coin, warmed by the fire, and hold it against the windowpane. The frost would melt in a tiny circle and each would peer through at the other, laughing all the while. The snow fell and piled high in the streets below and they longed to be together again but, until the snow melted, they could only peep through the tiny holes in the frosty glass. At last, the long spiky icicles would start to drip and the snows melt. Spring was coming and soon they would be together again in their garden.

Once again the warmth of the sun fell on them, and once again their love grew sweet as the roses twining above them. One sunny day a butterfly settled on Kai's finger. As the children wondered at its beauty, Kai gave a start: "Ouch," he said, making a face and clutching at his breast. The butterfly fluttered into the branches above them. "That hurt, whatever . . . Ouch!" A second time Kai cried out and this time he rubbed at his eye. "Something's hurt my eye, now!" he said.

"Let me look," said Gerda and her eyes were wide with care as she reached towards him.

"No, leave me be," snapped Kai and he pushed her away. It was the devil's splinters and they had entered his heart and his eye. Kai had never treated Gerda so roughly before and she started to cry.

"Oh, don't start blubbering," said Kai. "You look so ugly when you cry." He stood up and trampled on the new green herbs under his feet. "I'm fed up with this place," he scoffed. "Look at that worm-eaten rose,

. . . and there's another. I'm going!"
He kicked at the windowbox and
stamped away leaving Gerda alone to
her quiet tears in their broken garden.

Winter came again and the city was
covered once more in a white blanket of
snow. Each night Gerda made a peephole in
her window, but whenever she saw Kai, he
would turn away. She knew he still looked from
his window, but now, it was never for her. It was as
if she had become a stranger . . .

One night the snow was falling heavily, swirling and tumbling in the
gusty wind. Kai watched the snowflakes pile up on his windowsill, one
on top of the other and as he watched them settle, they formed
themselves into strange shapes. He looked more closely and before his
eyes the outline of a face began to form. He could just make out a pair of
deepset eyes beneath a high brow, a finely-chiseled nose and the thin
line of beautiful lips. The face seemed to be looking straight at him and
suddenly it came to life. Although a little afraid, Kai thought the face
very beautiful. The finely-drawn lips smiled at him but the smile had no
warmth in it – it was as cold as the frost of the darkest night.

The next day Kai felt bored. He didn't know what to do and was tired
of staying indoors. Finally, he asked his grandmother if he might take
his sled to the square to play with the other town boys. His tone was cross
and his face sullen.

"And Gerda," she asked. "Is she going too?"

Kai gave a sneer and walked over to the door and began to put on his
coat and gloves. "I won't be playing with her," he said. "She is just a silly
child. She spends her time moaning and crying." The door slammed and
he was gone. From her window Gerda watched him trudge through the
snow, dragging his little sled behind him. She felt a deep sorrow pierce
her heart – it seemed he no longer loved her.

In the square the tall buildings echoed as the town boys called to each
other, sliding back and forth on their sleds. Many of them held onto
passing carts to hitch a free ride, letting go just as the cart was about to
leave the square. Kai ran to join them and almost immediately a long
white sled pulled by two gray horses glided past him. The driver sat high
up in the front and was dressed from top to toe in the palest blue coat,
trimmed with the whitest fur Kai had ever seen. He watched as it

silently swished around the square and then, as it passed again, he leaped forward and tied his sled behind it.

Away they went at a fine speed. Kai hung on and laughed with delight as his little sled bumped and hissed through the thick snow. But then the big white sled began to move faster and turned to leave the square: it was heading straight for the city gates. Kai tried to untie the knot that bound the two sleds together but his fingers were numb and slow and he was forced to hold on even tighter lest he be thrown off and injured. He cried out but no one seemed to hear.

Faster and faster went the great sled and it seemed to Kai that they were flying through the snowdrifts. His teeth began to chatter and just when he thought he was about to fall, the great sled glided softly to a stop. Kai slumped down on his sled, exhausted.

The driver turned and for the first time Kai saw the face of a beautiful woman. Her skin was smooth and white and her eyes were an icy blue. She was looking down at him and Kai thought she reminded him of someone else. Was it the way she smiled? Where had he seen her before? he thought. Then he remembered the face in the snow. The face that he had seen outside his window. It was the Snow Queen!

She stepped down from her high seat and placed a hand on his shoulder. A chill ran through his body and he shivered.

"Are you cold, Kai?" she asked and she bent to kiss him. Her lips were as cold as ice and Kai felt a pain as sharp as a frozen needle stab through to his heart. When the chill of her kiss seeped through to the devil's splinter he felt the cold no longer. He was as ice himself.

"Come," said the Snow Queen. "Climb up beside me."

Kai could not believe how beautiful she was and wondered why he had thought her so cold and aloof; he had no doubts or fears now. He no longer cared where they were going and gave no thought to his home or his grandmother. He did not remember the roses or the love of his dear friend Gerda – all were now forgotten.

Swish went the sled across the icy wastes and then, rising into the air, it flew high above the ground. Kai looked down through the crisp, dark night and the dancing snowflakes: oceans and plains, snow-covered forests and jagged, white-topped mountains passed beneath him. Far below he heard the howling of wolves like the screech of the wind in his ears. They flew across a land of tumbling glaciers and black, cold waters until, at last, wrapped in the pure white fur of the Snow Queen's cloak, he fell into an icy sleep.

Meanwhile, in her tiny room, Gerda watched and waited for Kai's return. She had climbed up on her window seat and had sat there for hours peering through the frosty glass. At last, when he did not return, her tears began to fall. Oh, how she cried for her dear lost friend. Where had he gone?

The townsfolk said that by now he must have perished in the cold. Some of them had seen him leave the city behind the great white sled. Perhaps it had crashed through the ice while crossing the nearby river. Gerda's heart was full of sadness and each day, until the Spring returned once more, she watched from her window.

Then, as the first weak threads of early sunshine brushed her face she felt warm again. "My poor Kai must surely be dead," she murmured. But the sunbeams heard her soft voice and answered: "It is not so. It is not so."

The swallows swept and dove about her head and again Gerda said sadly: "Do you not know, my poor Kai is dead."

"It is not so. It is not so," they answered.

"Perhaps," said Gerda, taking heart, "my love is still alive. I will ask the river what it knows. I will wear my new red shoes for Kai has never seen them. I'm sure he'll think them pretty."

So Gerda put on the red shoes. They were simple and plain, but because she was so poor, she thought them beautiful and treasured them greatly. She crept downstairs and out of the house, crossed the great square and walked through the city gates. After a while she reached the wide river. It gurgled and swirled at her feet and she stood for a while watching the curling reeds waving under the clear water.

Gerda knelt down on the bank and looking deep into the water she asked: "Do you know if my Kai is alive? Please, if you can bring him back to me, I will give you my new red shoes."

The river sighed and Gerda thought she saw the reeds and the waters nod to her question. She unbuckled her shoes and threw them into the river. She was not very strong and her throw had cast them only a short way from the bank. The tiny waves lapped at the reeds and the shoes floated back as if the river was returning them to her.

"I have not thrown them far enough," she said and looking around she saw a boat nestled among the rushes. She climbed in and raising her arm high, she threw the shoes into the river again. This time they did not float back to her but her movement rocked the little boat and it began to move. Slowly, but surely, it drifted out from the bank. Gerda ran to the

back of the boat but it was too late: it was already too far for
her to jump to safety. There was nothing she could do.

Gerda huddled fearfully in the spinning boat as it moved faster and
faster. She drew up her knees and hugged herself but then the swallows
came again. "Do not cry," they said. "We are with you, don't be
frightened."

Their voices made her feel better and she sat up and looked around.
She was drifting through a land of green willow trees and tall rushes,
dipping and swaying in the warm summer breeze. Wild flowers,
sparkling like colored jewels, speckled the gently waving grasses of the
meadow.

"Perhaps I am being taken to Kai," she thought and she smiled
quietly to herself.

For many hours the boat drifted along on the rippling water. Gerda
sat and watched the scenery glide past but suddenly she saw a tiny
cottage. It had a pointed roof and two small windows made from
colored glass. Strangest of all, however, were two wooden soldiers
standing on either side of the doorway. Gerda called out to them and
they saluted but they did not answer. Fearful that she would be carried
right past the cottage she called out again. This time her cry brought an

old lady to the cottage doorway. She came over to the bank, took hold of the boat with her long crooked stick and drew it safely into the reeds.

"Why my poor little love," she said. "What are you doing so far from home?" The old lady was tall and thin, and on her head she wore a huge straw hat completely covered with flowers. They danced and played around its brim as she bobbed her head up and down. Gerda took her hand and jumped out of the boat. She felt a little uneasy as the old lady led her up to the cottage.

"Do you have a story to tell, my dear?" she asked, and Gerda told her of her search for Kai and of her long journey down the river. She then asked the old lady if she had seen Kai.

"Not yet, my pet," replied the old lady. "But he may pass my door some day and pay me a visit." The lady clapped her hands together: "Now," she said, "would you like something to eat? I have some cherries that are ripe and fresh and, afterwards you can see my garden. I have such lovely flowers planted there and should you ask them, each will tell you a different story."

Gerda entered the cottage and found a large bowl of cherries. She began to eat them. The sunshine darted through the colored glass of the windowpanes and made pretty patterns of red, blue and yellow all over the walls.

The old lady went to a drawer and took out a comb, then she began to comb Gerda's hair. "You are a pretty child," she cooed. "Such fine hair is rightly fit for my golden comb. A child like you has been my heart's desire. We shall surely come to love each other."

Gerda felt soothed by the old lady's soft voice and gentle stroking. She had eaten her fill and now her thoughts drifted away from her beloved Kai. She closed her eyes and listened to the soft buzz of the afternoon. She felt warm and drowsy and slipped into a light sleep.

The old woman was, indeed, a witch. But her magic was only used for good and not for evil; it had worked very well. She thought it very fortunate that Gerda had been brought to her door, now all she needed was to make sure that Gerda stayed with her. "I must make the child forget about her young friend, Kai," she murmured. And while Gerda slept the old lady went into her garden. She went straight to the rosebush and sweeping her stick over it, she whispered a magic charm. Instantly, the roses disappeared: the other plants closed up, leaving no trace of where the rosebush had been. "Now there is no flower in the garden to remind her of Kai," she said.

When Gerda awoke the old lady led her out of the house into the garden. The sun was shining and Gerda was astonished at how beautiful it was. She had never seen so many flowers and she knelt and played among them. Her heart was filled with delight at the sight of so much color and the scent of so many sweet perfumes.

One day followed another and Gerda spent all of her time in the enchanted garden among the flowers. But a tiny doubt had entered her mind. "They are not all here," she said. "But which flower is missing? I wish I could remember."

That evening, as the old lady sat in her large wicker chair, dozing contentedly, Gerda suddenly looked up and gasped. "The rose!" she cried, pointing at the old lady's hat. "That's the one that's missing!"

"Oh my, Oh my..." began the old lady, but it was too late: Gerda had seen the one single rose that had escaped the old lady's spell. Gerda realized at once that she had been deceived. She ran from the cottage and sank to her knees in the garden. She was so upset that she began to cry. Her tears fell to the ground and touched the spot where the rose bushes had once bloomed, instantly they sprang back to life. Gerda was overcome with joy. Taking a rose in her hand she wept bitterly: "Oh Kai, I so nearly forgot you. I have wasted my time with flowers when I should have been searching for you." She looked closely into the warm heart of the rose and asked: "Is my dear Kai alive? Have you seen him?"

The rose in her hand seemed to shiver: "No, I have not seen him and I know only too well of death, but nothing of Kai. He is surely alive." Gerda ran from flower to flower and asked them all the same question. "Is Kai alive? Is Kai alive? Have you seen him?" She heard many stories and strange tales but all of them turned away at her question and said they knew nothing of him.

"I cannot stop and listen to your tales," cried Gerda. "I must find Kai." And she ran from the garden and out through the gate. Finally, exhausted, she sank down to the ground and fell into a deep sleep.

When she awoke she shivered and hugged herself, it had grown quite chilly. Then she heard a strange sound.

"Coo-roo, . . . roo, roo! Coo-roo, . . . roo, roo!" There it was again. Just then a leaf fluttered down and landed in her lap; she looked up and there, perched in the branches of a tree, was a fat wood-pigeon.

"Hello," she said. "Is it Autumn already?"

"Why, yes," said the pigeon. Then Gerda remembered the garden; it was enchanted. No seasons affected the flowers there, no frosts drove the

plants underground for the winter, it had always been summer. "Please, have you seen Kai?" she asked and her voice was urgent. The pigeon paused and looked thoughtful, then he said sadly: "Yes, I have seen him . . ." His voice trailed off in a murmur. Gerda thought he was about to cry and fearing the worst she blurted out: "Is Kai dead?"

"No, he's alive. I was here by my nest a winter ago and I saw him pass overhead. He was with the Snow Queen in her sled." Once again the pigeon paused. "As she flew by," he went on, "she breathed an icy kiss on my young ones and they perished . . . every one."

The pigeon gulped and looked away. Gerda waited for a moment and then she asked in a softer voice: "Where were they going? I must find Kai." The pigeon shuffled his feet before answering.

"To Lapland. It's a long way from here, to the North . . . and very cold. I'm afraid I don't know the way, but if you ask the reindeer they'll be sure to tell you. Go north from here, only a short distance, and you'll come to the land where they live." Gerda thanked him and set off. She left the pigeon sadly staring off into the distance.

The farther north she went the colder it got. Patches of snow dotted the ground and Gerda's feet became frosty blue. At last she saw a reindeer scratching his back against a fallen tree trunk.

The reindeer, who had a kind face, listened patiently while Gerda told him her story. When she had finished he said that he would take her on his back to the land of the Snow Queen.

"Does she live in Lapland?" asked Gerda.

"Only in the summer," answered the reindeer. "Her winter palace lies far away to the north in a land of darkness and lights. Where the ice never melts and the wind cuts through you like a knife."

Gerda climbed onto his broad back. "It's getting cold," he said. "You'd better snuggle as deep as you can into my thick fur."

Off they went across the wide plain. The land grew white with frost and cold as ice. The reindeer galloped on and on and did not seem to notice the icy winds and tumbling snowstorms. All the while Gerda hugged herself closer and closer into his broad shoulders.

At last he came to a stop beside a ragged hut, its roof piled high with snow. The reindeer snorted two great puffs of steam and Gerda looked up. She could see the warm glow of a lamp shining from a tiny window. The door opened and an old Lapp woman peeped out. "Come inside, it's cold," she said, and the reindeer trotted into the hut.

He told the old Lapp woman Gerda's story. When he had finished she got up and fetched a bowl of steaming soup for Gerda and some fresh straw for the reindeer. After they had eaten she pulled a thick fur about her knees and began to talk. "Kai is living with the Snow Queen. He is deep inside her palace and he is content. To him it is the most beautiful place on earth. He does not feel the chill in his bones or the frost on his face. His heart is filled with ice and he is happy there. Unless the magic that has entered his eye and his heart is destroyed, he will never know what it is to be human again."

Gerda was near to tears when she heard the old woman's words. It seemed she had lost Kai's love forever.

"But what magic can bring him back, old woman?" asked the kindly reindeer, cocking his great antlers to one side. "What can Gerda do?"

"There is no magic," said the Lapp woman. "It is the warmth of Gerda's love that will bring Kai back from his frozen life. Has she not

traveled far in the hope of finding him? Has she not trusted the birds of
the air and the flowers of the field to guide her way? Such a faithful love
is all that can release him from his icy tomb."

"It is still far away," said the reindeer, "but I will take you to the
gates of the palace. I can go no farther, or I too, will perish."

The next morning at dawn, the old Lapp woman dressed Gerda in a
warm fur suit. Then she kissed her goodbye and they set off once more
across the frozen ice.

Gerda had never seen so much ice. It twisted and tilted in crackling
mountains of blue and white. The snow danced in a frenzy and the wind
screamed about their ears. The closer they got to the Snow Queen's
palace, the colder it became, until, finally, when it seemed the very air
itself was frozen, the reindeer stopped.

"We are here at last," he said and his voice was tired and weary.

"Thank you dear friend," said Gerda, and leaning forward, she kissed
him on top of his nose. The reindeer looked sad. "Good luck, Gerda," he
whispered.

Gerda left him at the palace gates. As she turned to wave two tears fell
from his large brown eyes and rolled down his shaggy cheeks.

Inside the palace the corridors and caverns glistened and sparkled. Icy creakings echoed through the bone-chilled chambers. Deep in its cold heart was the Snow Queen's throne room. There, seated on a throne of ice, encrusted with the frozen tears of a million sadnesses, sat the Snow Queen. Her gown was the color of the bluest iceberg, trimmed with frozen jewels as black as the polar sea; on her head she wore a crown of splintered ice needles.

On the floor at her feet sat Kai. He was playing with a pile of ice fragments, making up words: ICE, CHILL, DARKNESS, COLD . . . over and over again he spelled out the words. His hair was frosty white and his face and hands were an icy black. He was as cold as the Snow Queen's smile but he felt nothing. His brittle fingers toyed with the splinters, one word eluded him and his memory, for it was lost.

The Snow Queen had once told him of the word, it was ETERNITY: she had promised him his freedom if he found it among the fragments. But now, his fingers were so numb and his mind so frozen, that he could not remember a single letter.

Suddenly, the Snow Queen stood up and clapped her hands. Instantly her glistening sled appeared before her. She smiled at Kai as she stepped into her high seat. "I am going away for a while," she said. "I must tend to the snows on the tops of the volcanos. Their warmth is sometimes strong enough to melt the thickest ice and I must breathe on them again and cap them in white."

The sled hissed from the chamber and the crack of her whip echoed through the palace like a thousand snapping icicles. Kai was left alone, all was silent except for the tiny clinking of the ice splinters falling between his frozen fingers.

*   *   *

Gerda entered the chamber and the chill air cut through her cloak and gnawed at her bones. Then she saw the tiny figure by the throne. "Kai," she called. "At last I've found you. It's me, dearest friend, Gerda."

Kai turned but his face gave no sign of warmth. His cold blue eyes seemed not to know her. He did not move and his hands remained frozen at his side.

Gerda flung her arms around him and wept. "It's me, it's me, Kai," and the tears fell from her eyes. She felt the icy chill of his shoulders against her and the frozen stiffness of his body seeped through her thick fur suit. There was no response; it was as if he had no love for her at all. In despair, Gerda lowered her head to his breast and sobbed bitterly.

Her tears were warm and full of love and, falling on his breast, they entered his heart. The evil splinters melted in the flood of her love. She felt Kai stir; he stood back, holding her away from him as if to see her more clearly.

Gerda would have collapsed had he not held her shoulders. She looked sadly at him with eyes full of love and warmth. She had longed for him so much all through her long journey and now her tears ran freely down her cheeks. "It's Gerda. Don't you remember the roses?" and her sad voice was like a tiny sunbeam.

At that moment the warmth in Kai's heart flowed into his memory. Thoughts of their childhood came flooding back to him: it was Gerda! Seeing her dear face in front of him as if for the first time, his eyes filled with tears. He clasped her to him and cried so freely that his eye was washed clean of the devil's second splinter. He could see now the beauty of her smile and the dark ugliness all around him; he felt alive and he shivered as he became aware of the cold.

Gerda kissed him and kissed him and with every kiss more warmth flowed into his cold body. Their tears mingled and fell to the floor onto the ice splinters that lay there. Some of them were melted and some of them were frozen into new letters. Kai glanced down and saw the word ETERNITY. "We are free, my love," he said.

*   *   *

Full of joy they ran from the palace, through the frozen gates and onto the snow-covered wasteland outside. The terrible wind now seemed to be quieter and as they walked along a faint gleam of sunshine broke through the clouds and warmed their faces. They reached the top of a tumbling snowdrift and Gerda smiled: "Hello, old friend," she said. It was the reindeer.

"I, . . . I thought I'd wait around for a while," he muttered. "Just in case I was needed."

Together they climbed onto his broad back and set off for their home. It was a long way, but strangely the cold did not now chill them. The sun came out and in no time at all the snows had disappeared and they were riding into a green meadow. Here, the reindeer set them down and bade farewell. This time he smiled as he watched them go on their way.

Soon Kai and Gerda discarded their warm fur coats. The sun was shining and the sky seemed full of swallows. They darted and played, swooping down around the heads of the young couple.

"Did we not say. It was true. It was true," they whispered.

At last they saw in the distance the tall towers and steeples of Copenhagen. With their hands locked together they turned and looked into each other's eyes. No warmth could match the love they felt for each other. "Remember our roses?" said Kai gently, and he kissed her tenderly on the lips.

They were no longer children, but had grown, as had their love.

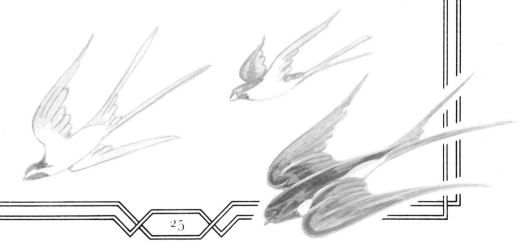

The Tinder Box

"ONE, TWO, THREE, FOUR! Left, . . . right! Tramp, tramp! One, two, three, four!"

"Good morning, handsome soldier," said a voice suddenly.

The soldier stopped abruptly. He was marching home from the wars and was absent-mindedly counting his footsteps and listening to the chink of his buckles and belts.

The voice came from an old witch sitting at the side of the road. Her lower lip hung way down below her long crooked nose and the soldier thought her extremely ugly.

"What a fine soldier you are," she said. "And what a bright sword and tidy pack you have. How would you like all the money you can carry?"

The soldier gulped. "Thank you very much, old lady," he stammered. "But what must I do for such wealth?"

The old witch stood up and her old bones creaked. She raised a bony finger and pointed to a nearby tree. "That tree is hollow; if you climb to the top and crawl into the hole, you can slide down inside it."

"But what for?" asked the soldier. "And how will I get out?"

"For the money, of course," cackled the old crone and her long lip quivered. "I will tie a rope about your waist and pull you up when the time is right." The old witch drew close beside him and wagged her finger under his nose. "Now," she croaked, "listen carefully. When you reach the bottom you will find yourself in a passageway lit by a hundred lamps: there you will see three doors. They lead into three chambers, each is locked, but you will be able to open them by turning the iron keys which are in place. Inside the first chamber you will see a chest and on the chest you will see a dog with eyes the size of teacups."

The soldier gulped again and looked a little worried.

"Don't worry about him, my lad," went on the witch, seeing his concern. "Here, take this blue check apron; if you place it on the floor

in front of the chest and lift the dog down onto it, then he will not harm you. Then you can help yourself to the coins in the chest. They will be copper, but if it's silver you prefer you must go into the next chamber. There, on a second chest you will see a dog with eyes the size of millstones. Place him on the apron and the silver will be yours for the taking. If silver is not to your liking and gold is your fancy, then you must enter the third chamber. There, on yet another chest will be another dog, but this one has eyes the size of the Round Tower of Copenhagen. Once again, all you need do is place him on my apron and he will not harm you. The gold will then be yours."

"Well," said the soldier, scratching his head. "That all sounds very reasonable to me." He paused and looked sideways at the old witch. "I daresay, though, that when I come out you will want a share of the money?" He raised his eyebrows quizzically.

"No," replied the witch hastily. "I want nothing of the gold, the silver or the copper. Just bring me the tinder box my grandmother left there when she last went into the tree – that is all I want from you."

"All right then, old lady," said the soldier. "Let's have your apron and the rope and I'll be about my duties." He tied the rope tightly round his middle and sprang up into the tree.

When he reached the top he climbed into the hollow and slid down and down until at last he dropped with a bump into a long passageway. Just as the witch had said, it was lit by a hundred lamps, and in front of him were three doors.

He opened the first door. There sat the dog with eyes the size of teacups and it was staring straight at him. "Golly," said the soldier and lifting down the dog onto the witch's apron he opened the chest. Inside, the copper coins gleamed brightly and he quickly filled his pockets to the brim, stuffing coins in until the pockets bulged.

Next, he opened the second door. "Well, I'll be blessed!" he exclaimed: there sat the dog with eyes the size of millstones. "You shouldn't stare," said the soldier. "It will make your eyes sore and besides, it's rude." He picked the dog up, placed him on the apron and opened the chest. When he saw the shining silver coins he emptied his pockets and let the copper fall to the ground. He refilled them with silver, stuffing the coins in as tight as they would go; for good measure he filled his pack as well: it was so full he couldn't fasten the buckles.

Then he went into the third room. There sat the dog with eyes the size of the Round Tower of Copenhagen. The soldier was astonished and a little bit afraid. For a brief moment he stood there rooted to the spot, but plucking up his courage, he saluted and said politely: "Good morning." The dog's eyes swiveled around like cartwheels as the soldier struggled to lift him onto the apron. He opened the final chest and it was filled to the brim with gold coins. There was more gold than he had ever seen in his life. Quickly, he replaced the silver coins with gold and stuffed them into his pockets, his pack, his hat, his socks and his boots and every other nook and cranny about his uniform; he even squeezed coins into his buttonholes. He replaced the dog on top of the chest and called up to the old witch: "You can pull me up now, old girl."

Her voice echoed back down the hollow tree, "Have you got the tinder box?"

"Oh, sorry, I nearly forgot," and the soldier went back for it, his boots clinking as he walked. The witch heaved and pulled and at last the soldier stood back on the road. Gold coins peeped out from his bulging pockets, from the top of his pack, from his boots and his hat – he felt very pleased with himself.

"Give me the tinder box," said the witch. Her tone was harsh and the soldier drew back.

"Why do you want it?" he asked, holding it close to his tunic. The witch made a clutching grab towards him. "It's none of your business," she snapped.

The soldier was beginning to get angry. "Tell me what you want it for, or I'll draw my sword and cut off your head."

"No, I won't," she screamed and curled her nails as if to tear out his eyes. The soldier drew his sword and with one stroke, cut off her head. Then, with the dead witch at his feet, he placed all the gold in the middle of her apron, tied the corners together into a fat bundle, and with the tinder box tucked in his breast pocket, set off for the nearby town.

29

When he reached the town he went to the finest inn and asked for the best rooms in the house. Then he ordered an enormous meal of all his favorite dishes. He had so much gold that he was rich enough to buy anything he wanted.

The very next day the soldier sent out for a new pair of boots and some fine clothes more suited to his new-found wealth. He stood in front of his mirror: "My word, what a fine gentleman I am."

The people of the town came to make his acquaintance. They told him all about their city, and of the king and queen, and of their lovely daughter, the princess.

"I would dearly like to meet her, she sounds so beautiful," said the soldier. "Is it possible to catch a glimpse of her in the castle grounds?"

"Oh no, that is impossible," replied the townsfolk. "Only her parents, the king and queen, are permitted to see her. They have shut her up in a great castle with high walls and many guards. It is foretold that she will marry a common soldier and the king lives in dread of the prophecy coming true."

"Well, it's a pity, such beauty . . ." murmured the soldier, reflectively, but he saw that it was unlikely he would ever see her.

The soldier lived comfortably. He had many friends and rode in a fine carriage. Although he enjoyed living like a lord, he never forgot what it was like to be down-and-out, and so he gave much of his money to the poor. Because of his generous nature it was not long before all his money was gone. His fine friends stopped coming to see him; he gave up his splendid rooms and was forced to move into a drafty attic at the top of the inn.

"Too many stairs to climb," grumbled his one-time friends and they turned up their noses as he passed.

He no longer had servants to polish his boots and wait on him; he had hardly any food to eat, and at night, when the cold wind blew through the rooftop, he would sit shivering in the dark because he could not even afford to buy the smallest lamp. One such night he remembered that he had seen a stub of candle lying in the bottom of the tinder box. It would brighten his room, he thought, and straightaway he took up the box, removed the candle and struck at the flint. As the tiny spark flew from the flint the door burst open and in bounded the dog with eyes the size of teacups. His glowing eyes lit up the room.

"Master, what is it you wish?" asked the dog.

The soldier was astonished. "Why," he stammered "that is surely a

very special tinder box, indeed!" After a moment he recovered from his surprise and said: "Good dog, you can bring me some money for a start." The dog ran out and in a flash was back with a bag of copper coins in his mouth; he laid them on the floor in front of his master.

"Aha, so that's it," said the soldier. It was now clear to him why the witch had so wanted the tinder box for herself. One strike on the flint brought the dog with eyes the size of teacups; two strikes brought the dog with eyes the size of millstones and three strikes brought the dog with eyes the size of the Round Tower of Copenhagen.

The soldier returned to his fine chambers and once again wore his expensive clothes. His old friends suddenly found him acceptable again. "What a fine fellow he is," they said, and they constantly fluttered around him.

The soldier, however, grew sad at times. He could not drive the princess from his thoughts. "If she is so beautiful, then why is she locked away? It is such a pity. How dearly would I like to see such beauty." This thought had hardly crossed his mind when it was replaced with another: "The tinder box!"

He reached out for the flint and struck it; immediately the dog with eyes the size of teacups was at his side. "I'm sorry to call you so late," said the soldier. "I would like to see the princess. Can you bring her to me?"

The dog grunted and was gone and back in the blink of an eye. There, fast asleep on his back, lay the beautiful princess. She looked so soft and lovely as she slumbered that the soldier could not resist gently kissing her. Then, with a sigh, he sent the dog away to return her to the castle.

The following morning, when the princess was at breakfast with the king and queen, she spoke of having a strange dream. In her dream a dog had carried her away on his back and a soldier had kissed her.

"Really, whatever next," snorted the queen, but she gave the king a sharp look and he, in turn, was looking very worried. That night a guard was posted outside the princess's door. "One can't be too careful," said the queen. "It may only have been a dream, but just in case . . ."

The soldier again sent for the princess, but although the whole town was asleep, the watchful guard was not. He followed the dog as it padded through the dark streets until he saw it enter the inn where the soldier lived. The crafty guard took a piece of chalk and drew a cross on the door of the inn: in the morning he would tell the king what had happened and, because of the cross, they would easily find the house again. The guard smirked and thought of his reward.

Much later when the dog returned from the castle, he noticed the white cross gleaming in the moonlight. He guessed what had occurred and being a very clever dog, he took up another piece of chalk and drew a cross on every door in the town. Now, should anyone try to find his master, it would be very difficult.

The next morning the king and queen, feeling very smug, set off with the guard and a host of servants to find the house marked with a cross. Hardly had they left the palace when the king exclaimed: "Aha! I've found it!"

"No dear," said the queen, looking a little pained. "Don't be silly. You have made a mistake. It is here."

"No, Your Majesty, it is here," said the guard.

"And here!"

"And here's another."

Wherever they looked they saw white crosses chalked on every door. The queen was very angry: she had been outwitted. Her eyes grew narrow and she thought very hard, wondering how to get her own back. At length she took up a square of fine silk and sewed it neatly into a small bag. This she filled with fine barley grain and then she tied it around the waist of the princess with a silken ribbon. While the princess was not looking the queen deftly took a pair of scissors and cut a tiny hole in the

bottom corner of the bag. It was just large enough for the tiny grains to fall, one at a time, to the ground. Should the princess again leave the castle, the grains would leave a trail and show the way she went.

That night the soldier again sent the dog for the princess. By now he loved her so deeply that his only thought was to make her his wife. If only he were a prince and not a common soldier it would be so easy. Alas, the dog did not notice the barley grains falling from the silken bag – in the morning the trail was clearly followed, the soldier was arrested and thrown into prison.

The unfortunate soldier slumped in his gloomy cell: he was to be hanged the very next day. In the confusion of his arrest he had forgotten to pick up the tinder box. Only that could save him now. How was he to get it?

At daybreak the soldier heard the far-off hammering as the carpenters built a gallows outside the city walls. He could hear the beat of drums and the tramp, tramp, tramp of the royal guards marching up and down. The time for the hanging was drawing close and people were scurrying all about the town getting ready to watch his execution. Suddenly, a boy ran past the window of his cell and lost one of his shoes. As he bent to pick it up the soldier called to him through the bars.

"Not so fast, my lad," he said urgently. "I'll give you five copper coins if you run to my house and fetch the tinder box you'll find there. But, you must run as fast as you can and waste no time at all."

The lad blinked and was off in a flash and back again before the soldier had counted to twenty. "That was quick," he said, taking the tinder box and he handed the boy five copper coins through the prison bars. The boy ran off well-pleased with his reward.

It was time for the execution. The soldier was taken from the town and led up the steps of the gallows. In front of him sat the king and queen. The queen looked especially pleased with herself and smirked and nodded to the assembled crowd. At either side sat the royal judges and the council and the nobles of the court. Everybody waited.

The noose was placed around his neck but just as the hangman drew it tight the soldier raised his hand. "Wait!" he cried, stepping forward. Addressing the king he said that there was a tradition which allowed a condemned man a last request. May he, he asked, have the pleasure of one last pipe of tobacco.

The queen snorted indignantly but the king could not refuse.

The soldier took the tinder box from his pocket and struck it: once, twice, three times! In a flash the three great dogs appeared before him. One with eyes the size of teacups, one with eyes the size of millstones and one with eyes the size of the Round Tower of Copenhagen.

"Help me," cried the soldier. "I am to be hanged and I am innocent of any crime. I do not want to die!"

A low growl rose from the throats of the three dogs and they sprang into action. They bounded towards the judge and the council, picked them up in their snarling jaws and hurled them so high into the air that when they hit the ground their bodies broke into tiny pieces.

"Oh no, not me, I'm the king. You can't do that to me," whined the

king. But his protests were in vain and he fled in terror.
He was chased by the largest dog, with eyes the size of
the Round Tower of Copenhagen. He snatched up the king and queen
together and hurled them even higher into the air. The royal guards
were so afraid that they ran away in all directions.

Suddenly the crowd began to chant: "Soldier! Soldier! Be our king!
Marry the fair princess! Soldier be our king!"

He stepped down from the scaffold and was lifted high onto the
shoulders of the crowd. They carried him to the royal carriage and they
rode into the town. The great dogs barked and bounded about and
everybody cheered and whistled.

The beautiful princess came to the gates of the castle and the soldier
took her in his arms. They were married without further delay and the
wedding feast lasted for a whole week. Everyone had plenty to eat
especially the three great dogs. They rolled their great eyes and kept a
careful watch over their master and his beautiful new bride.

The Little Mermaid

HAVE YOU HEARD, that deep in the sea, live the mer-people? They live where the ocean is the bluest of blues and as deep as twenty mountains, piled one on top of the other.

At the deepest, bluest part is the palace of the mer-king. Its walls are built of crimson and white coral and its roof is tiled with lustrous oyster shells which sparkle as their tiny pearls blink in the filtering sunbeams. Tall windows, laced with the finest fan coral, gleam with the glow of pure amber taken from the belly of a whale. The palace stands in the center of a great forest of tall trees and thickly clustered bushes, curling and waving in the tilting waters. Fishes, stranger than any you can imagine, slip through the branches and leaves; brightly-colored flowers open and close as they sift the tide and the painted shells of a thousand creatures line the byways.

The king's dear wife had long since died and now the palace was cared for by his mother. She was kind and thoughtful and was all but a mother to the king's six daughters. They were the fairest princesses in the sea, but the most beautiful was undoubtedly the youngest. Her skin was as soft as the bloom on a rose and her soft eyes were a deep sapphire blue. Of course, like all mermaids, she had no legs, instead, her slender body tapered down into a graceful tail.

Their lives were full of play: they would swim and dart among the trees swirling up the soft silver sand. The sun was their delight and they played in its dappled beams as it filtered through the giant fans, flooding the palace gardens in golden light.

At times the sisters would gather at their grandmother's tail and listen to stories of the land above the water. Their eyes grew wide as she told of ships and men, cities and towns; of creatures called birds that swam through the trees like fishes; of animals with hair and horns that prowled the shoreline and of flowers that filled the air with the sweetest

of perfumes. The youngest mermaid opened her eyes wide.

"Can I see for myself, Grandmama?" she begged, and flipped her tail excitedly. Her grandmother chuckled and drew them close.

"Not yet, my children," she said softly. "When you are fifteen, then it will be time. Then you can swim to the top of the sea and watch the ships go by. Close to the shore you'll see cities and trees, but take care when you go that near."

Must she wait that long thought the youngest. There was a span of five years between her and her eldest sister and she longed for the time to pass quickly; to the day when she would be fifteen.

She was a passive gentle creature and at night she would wait and peer up at the moon. Its great silver bowl would glimmer down into the cool, blue depths and the stars would shiver and twinkle around it. Sometimes a sail would go shadowing by and she wondered what beings kept watch on its decks. Did they know she was there? . . . Waiting.

As year followed year her sisters swam to the shore, and each had returned to tell what they'd seen. One heard the music of church bells chiming; one saw an arrow of wild swans swooping; one saw swimming children and wanted to play, but a dog had appeared and chased her away; the fourth stayed at sea for she had more care, but the dolphins had come and leaped in the air; the fifth sister went where the winter seas ran and sat on an iceberg all through the night, while the ships short-sailed by and their sailors took fright.

The little mermaid was overwhelmed by their stories, but her sisters soon tired of the land and spent their time in the palace gardens, so she heard no more of their tales. At times, though, they would leave her, lonely and sad, and swim off together. They would ride on the tall foaming waves and sing to the seamen on the storm-tossed sailboats. No sailor would dare answer their call, for fear of drowning.

At long last the day of her birthday arrived: she was fifteen! Now, she too, could swim to the land at the top of the sea. Her grandmother gave her a wreath of fine pearls to braid in her hair. She kissed her and took her hand. "Farewell, my little one," she said. "Take care."

The little mermaid smiled at her grandmother and then at her sisters. "Farewell," she said and with a last flip of her tail she rose up through the waters like a sparkling bubble.

Up and up she went until at last the water around her became clear and golden. She was almost at the top of the sea, then, in a blaze of shining, sun-drenched droplets, she burst through the surface.

The rim of the sun was just dropping beneath the nodding waves.
The sea was the color of the darkest rose, streaked with gold and the
palest jade. She looked around her and close by saw the tall gray shadow
of a three-masted ship. It lifted gently to its anchor on the evening swell
and its spidery rigging ran up and down between the tall black masts.
High up, one sail remained unfurled and men were dangling their feet
from the yard. She heard music drifting over the water and saw more
men dancing on the deck. As darkness closed in, lights appeared all over
the ship and blinked like colored stars.

The little mermaid swam closer to the great stern where lamplight
flickered over the dark water. She peeped in from the crest of a wave and
saw a large, richly-paneled cabin. Inside, she saw many people, finely
dressed and laughing, but one among them caught her eye. He was
young and handsome with kind dark eyes: he was, indeed, a prince and
tonight was his sixteenth birthday. The music and dancing was all part
of the celebrations.

After a while he left the cabin and went up on deck, the others
following close behind him. She swam round the ship, but suddenly the
sky was filled with a million colored stars. They fell around her and
hissed as they hit the water. She was so alarmed she flipped her tail and

slipped beneath the surface. After a moment she cautiously popped her head up again.

It was the first time she had seen fireworks and she marveled at the great display. As each one flared the darkness vanished, but just as soon, as each flame died, the night returned. Her eyes fell once more on the face of the prince, he was so young and handsome.

The night drew on and one by one the lamps went out, but the little mermaid stayed close to the ship hoping to catch just one more glimpse of the prince. Suddenly, as the sea lifted and settled beneath her, she felt a deep rumbling moan come up from the depths of the ocean. Black clouds began to tumble above her: a storm was coming. In an instant the sailors scurried back on deck, scrambled into the rigging and let loose the sails. The anchor chain clanked its way on board and the ship gurgled and hissed as it started to move slowly through the inky waters.

It picked up speed and the little mermaid swam faster to keep up with it. Lightning flashed and thunder echoed through the mountainous black clouds. The waves climbed higher and higher and crashed and pounded against the ship as it plowed along. One after another the sails were taken in until, in the boiling sea, the ship sailed on with her bare masts flailing the sky like great black bones.

The little mermaid swished and dived through the huge breaking rollers and played in the foaming spindrift; the sailors, however, were white with fear. Suddenly, a giant wave lifted the ship high in the air and as it dropped back, it pitched violently. With a splintering crack the mainmast snapped, swayed and crashed overboard, dragging the stricken ship onto her side. A second great wave rose up and crashed on to the decks, washing the ship from stem to stern and tearing its timbers to pieces. All the lights went out and at last the little mermaid saw the peril that faced the ship and her crew. Fear swept into her heart as spars and timbers slashed through the raging waters and threatened to crush her as she swam alongside. A flash of lightning split the darkness and in its glare she saw the broken ship rolling to its death. The poor wretched seamen were clinging to the tangled ropes that whipped about in the

screaming gale. They were going to drown and she scoured the deck for
sight of the prince. Then, with one last shuddering groan, and a terrible
tearing of timbers, the ship rolled over and slid beneath the boiling sea.

"He must not die," thought the little mermaid and she dove among
the tangled wreckage that surged and crashed around her. She searched
and searched and just when she was in despair of finding the prince, she
came upon his body. His strength was gone and his eyes were closed; a
moment more and he would have slipped beneath the wind-lashed
waves. She reached out and lifted his head above the foam. The sea
rolled and surged and took them on its course.

When daybreak came the storm had passed. The sun came up and shed an angry orange glow across the still wild rollers. The prince lay as if asleep in her arms and she gently kissed his brow. Tenderly she kissed him again and hoped with all her heart that he would live.

As the sun climbed higher the waves grew quieter and the little mermaid looked around. In the distance a range of snow-capped mountains loomed grayly over the horizon. She swam towards them and as she got nearer she saw the thickly wooded mountain slopes sweeping down into a green fertile valley. Among a grove of orange trees stood a white-washed building – she was unsure whether it was a church or a house. A small sheltered bay opened up as she swam closer and, gently supporting the prince, she rippled through the clear water and rested his head on the warm silver sand. She was careful to place him well beyond the reach of the tide.

Alone now, she swam away, but she had not gone far when she heard the sound of bells chiming. She turned and saw a group of young girls come out of the white building, which was in fact a church. They laughed and skipped into the garden surrounding it.

She swam swiftly to a rocky islet and watched and waited, not once did she take her eyes off the still figure of the prince.

One of the girls wandered close to the shore and seeing the prince lying on the sand, cried out and ran towards him. Soon, many people had gathered around him and as she watched, he sat up and smiled. He did not look out to sea at all and was unaware that it was the little mermaid who had saved him. She watched them carry him into the church and then, slipping from her hiding place, she dove down into the ocean and swam sadly back to her home.

The little mermaid's sisters asked her again and again what wonders she had seen, but her dreamy head could think only of the prince and of her kisses on his brow and she remained silent.

As day followed day she would swim to the tiny bay where last she'd seen him: the snow on the mountains melted, the trees flowered and bore their fruit, but despite her vigil, she saw no further sign of him.

At last she spoke to her eldest sister and to her surprise she discovered that her sister had not only heard of the prince but had often seen his ship. Once, she said, she had followed it right to the shore where it had anchored beneath a castle. Her sister took her hand and together they swam to the prince's castle. It towered above them on a needle of green rock and from its walls a staircase twisted down to the water's edge.

From then on the little mermaid went frequently to visit the castle. A wide balcony overhung the sea and she would swim beneath it, hoping to catch a glimpse of the prince in his home. She heard the sound of mens' voices and sometimes when he was not there, they would speak of him: how kind and generous he was, how thoughtful and caring for his people and how noble was his spirit. Her admiration for these strange beings increased daily and she wished more and more to become like them and share their land.

There came a day when she was no longer content to watch and wait and she went to her grandmother – she alone could tell her of the land above the sea.

"I know that men drown, Grandmama, but should they not, do they live forever?" she asked. "Or do they die someday, like us?"

Her grandmother smiled and answered in a soft voice. "Child, such a question. Yes, my dear, men die – and sooner still than us. We can swim through our lives for a full three hundred years, but the lives of men are but a quarter of that time. When a mermaid dies we become mere foam to cap the waves – just an added sparkle on the water, but that is all. With men it's different: they possess a spirit soul that rises up to fly among the stars and lives forever in a heavenly kingdom."

"Oh, if only it could be like that for me," said the little mermaid. "I would gladly give my three hundred years for just one day as a human being – to walk among their forests and explore their land."

An anxious look flickered across her grandmother's face. "No little one, you should not wish for such a thing. Our lives are happy here in the ocean but men have burdens we could not bear."

"But will I never see the heavenly land, Grandmama? Will I just

become drifting foam and never feel the warm sun on my face again? Is there nothing I can do to become human?"

Her grandmother took her hand and said gently: "The only way, my child, is for a man to love you more than his own life; when his every thought is of his love for you; then he will take your hand like this and let his soul pass into you. But, no man could love a mermaid. Your beautiful tail would seem absurd to him, no prettier than that of a fish – they do not see beauty as we do."

*　　　*　　　*

Some time later the little mermaid sat at the foot of the palace wall beneath a fathom of sadness. In despair, her thoughts turned to the sea witch: she must have courage and visit the terrible witch to ask for help. A tremor of fear snaked up her long tail and made her shudder.

She set out and swam to a far-off part of the ocean: it was strange to her and she became afraid. Nothing grew here and the water began to swirl and whirl about her; the colorful plants and the fish had vanished and it became a land of slimy darkness. She came at last to the enchanted forest that surrounded the home of the witch. It was not a forest of trees, but one of giant worm-like creatures that squirmed and oozed, back and forth, in the inky waters. They would trap and hold anything that came within reach of their writhing, sucking arms.

For a moment she feared to go on, but then she tucked her flowing hair tightly in her pearly headband and, with her arms held close to her sides, she sped through the blind, groping branches. All around she saw their wretched spoils: sea chests, barrels and cannon; drowned seamen, waving, ghastly, white-boned shadows; animals from the stricken ships that foundered above, eaten and bleached in their death-grip; and worst of all, the tangled yellow hair of a young mermaid, strangled and swaying in the murky tide.

After what seemed an age of twisting through the evil worms, she suddenly swam into a clearing. It bubbled and dripped with ooze and slime and in the center the sea-witch had built her house; it was made from the skulls and bones of shipwrecked sailors. There sat the witch and the little mermaid had never seen such ugliness. The witch's bloated body was covered with scales and her hair writhed like a thousand worms. White-bellied eels wriggled about her slimy tail, snails crawled on her face and breasts and in her lap sat a bulging sea-slug.

"I know your wish," she gurgled. "It is that of a fool, but I can satisfy your desire, . . . if only to bring you pain." The witch opened her sticky

mouth and a burbling cackle rose from deep in her throat: her body shook and shivered and some of the snails fell from her skin.

"A potion will I mix," went on the witch. "Drink it and you will have your stumps, your legs; your tail will split and there they'll be. But though you will walk and dance like an angel, every footstep will cut you like a thousand knives and your feet will flow crimson with blood." The witch's face grimaced into a smile: "Then let the prince fall in love with you!" She paused, "well, do you still wish to walk as a human?"

"Yes, I do," answered the mermaid nervously, and her thoughts of the handsome young prince gave her added strength.

The evil witch leaned her ugly head closer. "Remember well, Mermaid," she hissed. "Once a human, always a human! You may never be a mermaid again, nor swim, nor see your family and share their lives. Also, should you fail to enchant the prince and he does not take you as his wife and love you truly, then you will never gain an immortal soul. Nor will it end there, for should he take another for his bride, then your heart will break and you will die. Just one night should they spend together and you will turn to foam."

The little mermaid trembled but she nodded her head in agreement.

"No so fast, my pretty. What of my reward?" And the sea-witch sneered. "I demand a high price from you, little thing. I'll have your voice, the sweetest in the ocean, that is my price."

"But without my voice how can I talk with the prince and win his love?" The little mermaid grew fearful and her eyes grew wide.

The sea-witch was getting impatient and her hair writhed angrily.

"Your body will talk for you; your grace and slender form will charm a human heart. It will be my blood, cut from my veins, that seals the potion and gives it the power you need. But first, I'll have that tongue of yours." She leaned forward and gurgled spitefully.

The witch curled her evil body over a swirling cauldron and the potion was mixed.

The little mermaid took the potion from the witch. It was like crystal clear water. She gave no thanks, she was mute and could neither sing nor speak. She swam quickly away from the dreadful place and turned towards the prince's castle. On her way she passed the sleepy palace of her father. She thought fondly of him, her dear sisters and her loving grandmother. She was full of sadness and raised her fingers to her lips to blow them one last kiss.

*   *   *

She reached the prince's castle just before daybreak; peeped above the pale, moon-kissed waters and swallowed the potion. Instantly, a frightful pain, like a red-hot knife blade, shot through her body and she fainted on to the cool sand of the shore.

The morning sun crept up the sky and as its rays swept over the beach, they warmed her face. She awoke and saw a handsome figure with coal-black eyes standing in front of her: it was the prince. Startled, she looked down at herself; she was naked and her tail was gone, in its

place were slender legs. Nervous and abashed, she covered herself with her golden hair.

"Who are you? How have you come to this place?" asked the prince. The sadness in her deep blue eyes was her only answer for she could not speak. He took her hand to lead her to the castle, but as soon as she stood, the witch's words came back to her. In truth, with each step, her feet were slashed by a thousand knives. She suffered the terrible pain in silence and stepped lightly alongside the prince.

In the castle she was dressed in fine silk and soft muslin. She sat in the court and minstrels played while slave-girls sang. One girl sang so sweetly that the prince applauded loudly and the little mermaid feared his attention would be only for her.

But then the slave-girls started to dance and whirled around the court. The little mermaid stood up and glided out among them. The others drew back as she tip-toed and danced lightly to the music: such grace and charm of movement were superb to see. She floated like thistledown: every movement of her delightful body emphasized her exquisite form. On and on she danced and the audience was thrilled. The prince became more and more enchanted but he did not know that with every step she took, a pain to match a razor's slash seared her feet.

"You are a delight!" he cried. "You will stay with us forever. You are my little foundling" – and he laughed kindly at her.

He took her riding through the deep cedar forests and into the sun-dappled groves of scented pines. Wild herbs filled the air with their heady fragrances and the sky was full of birdsong. They climbed high into the mountains, so high that they were able to look down onto the wispy white clouds. And all the while her feet were cruelly wounded, yet her love for the prince gave her strength and wherever he led her she smiled and followed.

At night she would climb down the marble staircase and bathe her injured feet in the moon-rippled sea. The cool water eased her pain and she let it trickle through her fingers. Suddenly, she heard singing, it was full of sadness and looking up she saw her sisters far out over the water. They waved to her and told of the sorrow her departure had brought to their lives. Each night after that, they came again, and sometimes brought her grandmother and her father with them. They never ventured close but stood far out across the dark rolling waves.

As the days passed, her love for the prince grew stronger. She would look into his face and search his eyes for love, but all she found was fondness. Why could he not love her and make her his wife? Would she never gain an immortal soul? Alas, the prince loved her as he would a child; she was the gentlest girl he knew and he would kiss her brow.

"Your dear sweet face reminds me of another," he said. "Once, long ago, I was shipwrecked and cast upon the shore. It was close to a convent and a girl who studied there, tended me and made me well. It is as though my heart can only love that girl, but I fear I will never see her again."

The little mermaid sighed and turned her eyes sadly away. "He does not know that it was I who saved him from the storm," she thought. "He does not know that it was I who kissed him tenderly and bore him up in the cruel waves and laid his dear head on the warm white sand. Should he not see her again, then perhaps he will grow to love me one day, instead. I will love him more and pray that day will come."

* * *

"It's about time the prince found a wife and settled down," said the king. "He will be married!"

The news spread quickly around the city, and all, save the prince, were excited by it. His heart was not in it, but he would obey his father's wishes and seek a bride. He went into the castle garden with the little mermaid and took her face in his hands.

"Little foundling," he murmured. "My one true love is far away and I

shall never see her again. But I have you always by my side to remind me of her, so come with me and help me find a suitable princess to marry. In truth, should I ever marry, I should choose you, for you are the sweetest, dearest one I know."

They sailed away and the prince spoke to her of the ocean. She listened attentively but inside she smiled to herself. Even had she been able to speak, she would have remained silent, for she knew more of the

ocean's secrets then he could imagine.
After many days the ship sailed to a stop
and let slip its great iron anchor. Ashore,
the town was bustling. Church bells rang
and children sang; banners flew from every
flagpole; grand feasts were laid out; soldiers
tramped smartly up and down and polished
their buttons, and people danced through the
streets in preparation for the wedding of the
prince to their lovely princess.

But the princess was not due to arrive until the following day. She had
been away, studying, at a convent by the sea!

It was, indeed, the same girl the prince had fallen in love with so long
ago. It was she who had found him on the beach and cared for him.
When the princess arrived the little mermaid saw that she was, without
question, very beautiful. Her long dark hair shone like burnished ebony
and her lovely face was as fair as the palest rose petal.

"Oh how happy I am," cried the prince taking hold of the princess's
hand. "I have found my one true love at last. And you, little foundling,
shall share my joy, for no one loves me more dearly than you."

The little mermaid knelt and kissed his hand; she held it close to her
cheek for a brief moment, her heart was close to breaking and her love
for him was like a thousand sorrows. Soon, when he wed, she would die
and tumble among the foaming waves.

The day of the wedding arrived and the bells chimed across the land.
Inside the great cathedral where the ceremony was taking place, the tall
silver candlesticks guttered and glowed on the rich tapestries hung on
the walls; the great organ peeled and boomed and a vast crowd was
seated to witness the affair. Alone, and kneeling close behind the
wedding couple, was the little mermaid. She was dressed in rich robes of
crimson silk and gold, but she saw and heard nothing. Her heart was full
of love for her lost prince and of tomorrow, when with the dawn, she
would die.

As dusk settled, the bride and bridegroom boarded the great ship.
The sails were let fly from the yards and it glided out onto the silver-
black sea. On the main deck a tent had been raised for the young couple
and beneath its scarlet and gold awnings was laid a quilt of the softest
down: here the prince and his beautiful bride would sleep that night.

When darkness came the lamps were lit all about the ship and the sailors broke into a merry dance. It was so like that other evening long ago when first the little mermaid had swum to the top of the sea. Now, she danced as never before. Her grace was matchless and her step as light as a butterfly. Her feet were still cut by a thousand knives but she no longer felt the pain: no pain could match the sorrow in her heart.

This was her very last night and her head was full of sad memories. Her dear, beloved prince would never know of her sacrifice: the loss of her voice, her sisters, her father and grandmother, and her constant terrible pain.

When the wedding couple retired for the night, the dancing stopped and the ship became quiet – only the helmsman at his creaking wheel and the little mermaid remained awake. She sat in the shadows high in the prow and watched for the first threads of dawn. Her sisters rose out of the waves and she saw that their heads had been shorn of their long flowing hair. Their oyster-pale faces looked up and were sad. "The sea-witch will help you, dear sister. You need not die. Here is a dagger she gave us; you must take it and pierce the heart of the prince and let his blood wash over your feet. Then you will have a tail again and can swim with us deep in the sea for the three hundred years that we have. Her price was our hair but we do not care."

The waves tumbled by and they cried out once more. "Hurry, dear sister, daybreak is close. Either you or the prince must die before dawn. Quickly, the sun is about to awake."

The breeze sighed and her sisters disappeared. The little mermaid picked up the dagger and softly drew back the curtain of the tent. The handsome prince and his lovely bride were sleeping peacefully. Kneeling beside him, she leaned over and kissed him tenderly on the forehead. Her hand clasped the dagger tight to her breast as she looked down on him; how fine he was, so young and strong. His eyelashes flickered and he stirred. Softly, and very gently, she kissed him farewell and left the tent.

She walked to the rail and flung the dagger as far out as she could into the lightening sea. As it sank, the sea around it turned red, as though stained with the blood from a broken heart.

Gray dawn streaked over the waters to the bounding ship and the

wavetops were tinged with the palest pink. The little mermaid turned and looked once more at the sleeping prince, but her dear love's face grew hazy as the mist of death clouded her dying eyes. She threw herself into the surging waves, her body grew light and she became the tossing foam of the sea.

*   *   *

The sun peeped its dish over the lip of the waves and sparkled warmly on the singing foam. The little mermaid no longer felt any pain, nor did she feel death. She could see the gold of the sun and feel the comfort of its warm arms around her. It seemed to be lifting her high into the clear, morning sky. All around her, flying and floating, were the airy forms of a thousand beautiful spirits. They were singing sweetly, but so softly that no human being could hear their voices: it was just like the breeze humming over clear crystal waters and rippling on the warm silver sand. She was as they were, a drifting spirit.

"Where am I?" she said, and her voice was the singing of pearls.

"Little mermaid," breathed the spirits, "we are the daughters of the air. You cannot gain your immortal soul without the love of a human being. But, like those of us who still wait, you can gain a soul by goodness and caring for others. Carry the fragrance of flowers to those that are sick; blow hard on the mists to dispel the illness held within; lift up the swallows from below, so that those on earth will marvel at their flight – do all of these things for three hundred years and you will find your soul. Your pain and the pure love of your heart is why you are here."

The sun was now high and she felt its warmth on her face, then, for the first time, a tear rolled down her lovely cheek.

Down on the sea she saw the ship plunging on; she could hear the seamen waking and calling. The prince and his bride stood by the rail and seemed to know she had returned to the sea. Unseen, she drifted down and kissed him; a zephyr of love brushed his cheek.

Then she flew with the others up into the blue summer sky. "In three hundred years I will see the heavenly kingdom," she murmured happily.

"Yes, or sooner still, my child," whispered the spirits. "When you drift to the bed of a sleeping child and smile an unseen smile, a year will be saved from the three hundred term, but a single tear adds a day."

The Little Match Girl

LONG, LONG AGO ON NEW YEAR'S EVE, it began to snow. It was the very last hour of daylight and people were scurrying about the town anxious to get home before dark and out of the dreadful cold.

As night fell, a poor little match girl trudged through the swirling snowflakes. She had no hat for her head and her feet were bare. She shivered as she struggled through the cold, dark streets and her feet became sore and frozen by the icy snow on the ground. Her hands were thrust deep into her apron pocket, clutching her bundle of matches, but the icy wind cut through the thin cloth and chilled her tiny fingers to the bone. Not one penny had she earned all day, no one had stopped to buy her wares and not one match had she sold.

"What shall I do?" she murmured and her lip trembled at the thought of her cruel father. "He will surely beat me for not selling any matches. I cannot go home." She shivered even more as she thought of the attic where she lived, right up under the snow-covered roof: so full of holes and cracks that the icy wind and snow screamed right into her room.

Her golden hair fell about her shoulders and sparkled like frost as the snowflakes settled on her head. She passed between the tall houses and from the lighted windows she heard laughter and caught the smell of food cooking. It was New Year's Eve and she was so hungry.

"If only I had a home so warm – and food to eat."

At last she slumped to the ground, sheltered from the tumbling snow in a narrow alleyway. Huddled close against the wall, she tucked her feet up beneath her ragged skirt to warm them. She clenched her tiny hands around the bundle of matches. "If only I dare light one," she thought. "It will warm me." She took a match and struck it – it flared up brightly and warmed her frozen fingers like a tiny sun. She gazed into the glowing flame and it seemed to become a blazing iron stove. She

stretched out her feet towards it, but suddenly she was in darkness
again, holding the burned-out match. The stove had disappeared.

She struck a second match. It burst into flame and cast a glow on the
wall in front of her and it seemed that she could see right through it.
Inside was a table laid for dinner: a pure white tablecloth, fine china,
sparkling silverware and tall elegant glasses. In the center of the table
was a grand roast goose surrounded by baked apples and juicy prunes.
As she watched the goose got up and even though it was pierced by a
knife and fork, it walked towards her. Hardly had she raised her hand to
greet it when the flame of the match died and her raw fingers felt the
cold, hard stone of the wall.

She fumbled for a third match and struck it. This time, as it flared into life, she found herself beneath a tall Christmas tree. Her eyes opened wide as she peered up through the greenery. Lighted candles flickered on every branch and gaily-colored dolls and toys were hung among them. She smiled softly, but then once more, the match went out. The candles that she'd seen were only the stars shivering above her. One of them began to fall and as she watched, it traced a thread of gold across the dark sky.

"Someone is dying," she whispered sadly. Her dear grandmother had told her so before she died – a shooting star was a soul on its way to heaven.

Her grandmother filled her thoughts – how kind she had been and how much she had loved her. She took another match and struck it. In its light she saw her grandmother. "Oh grandmother," she cried and stretched her arms towards her. "Please take me with you. I know you will surely disappear when the match burns out, just like the stove and the goose and the Christmas tree. Oh, please don't go."

As fast as her frozen hands would allow, the little girl took all her remaining matches and struck them, one after another: so dearly did she want her grandmother to stay with her. The matches flared as bright as a summer's day and she felt her grandmother's arms around her, lifting her up and away to a place where she no longer felt cold, or hungry or afraid. The little girl closed her eyes.

*   *   *

In the first gray light of dawn the little child was found. She had frozen to death, but on her face was the lingering trace of a smile. So happy had she been with her dreams.

The wintry sun shone down on the lifeless bundle huddled in the alleyway and around her feet were scattered the burned-out matches.

The Wild Swans

IN THE WINTER, when the snows come, the swallows fly away to a far off land. In that same land, and long ago, there lived a king who had eleven sons and one beautiful daughter whose name was Elise. All the king's children were very content, but alas, their happiness was not to last.

Their mother had died some years before and now the king had decided to marry again. However, he chose the hand of an evil queen who was quite unlike their own kind mother. On the day of the wedding, when the children expected to share the feast, she sneered and gave them a bowl of sand instead of food.

Her wickedness knew no limit and it was not long before she sent Elise away from the palace to live with a poor peasant woman, and not content with that, she whispered falsehoods to the king about his eleven sons. Sadly, the king believed her lies and grew cold towards them.

The queen became impatient and wanting the palace to herself, she spoke angrily to the princes. "Go away," she snarled, "and look to yourselves. Fly now, fly, as birds that have no voice." Her curse took effect and the eleven brothers became eleven pure white swans. Only during the hours of darkness could they be as men again. The stricken princes wheeled their white wings into the air and with a last eerie cry they flew from the palace.

They flew far across the wide forest until, below them, they saw the humble cottage where Elise was sleeping. They circled and swooped in the dawn sky, beating their wings and trying to peep through the tiny window of her room. But it was all in vain for no one saw them and Elise slept on peacefully. At last, they gave up and soared high above the clouds. On they flew across the great forest until, leaving the land, they reached the waters of the ocean. Far out they flew until, just before the sunset, they dipped their wings over the horizon and disappeared.

Rose and briar grew close about the cottage where Elise lived and soft breezes played among them. "Rose so fair," whispered the wind. "Who is more beautiful than you?" But the roses only trembled and answered in one word: "Elise." And the breeze brushed the old lady's hair as she sat with her prayer book. "Good prayer book, who is as saintly as you?" And again the wind was answered: "Elise," said the book.

Elise missed her dear brothers, but time went by. As she grew older she became slender and beautiful; her skin was fair and her hair was long and golden. At last when she was fifteen, she was summoned to the palace, but the evil queen took one look at such delicate beauty and seethed with hate and jealousy. Her cruel heart craved to turn Elise into a swan like her brothers, but her fear of the king's anger prevented her. He had given the order for Elise to be brought back and the queen did not dare go against his wishes.

However, the queen was set upon revenge and went to the palace bathroom. There, among the carpets and couches spread on the marble floor, she took three toads from her gown and kissed them, one by one.

"Go sit on the head of the fair Elise, that she may be dulled and as dim as you.

"Make your seat on her brow that her face may be shriveled and as ugly as yours, that the king may not know her.

"Take rest on her breast that her heart becomes black and as wicked as yours, and let's not forget that she must feel pain."

Thus did the queen instruct the three toads as she slipped them into the bath water.

The queen then sent for Elise, undressed her and helped her into the bath. At once the three toads settled on her graceful body; one on her head, one on her brow and one on her breast. Elise paid them no attention and seemed not to notice. When she rose from the water the toads had vanished: in their place floated three scarlet poppies. Her purity and innocence had overcome the queen's evil power.

When she saw that her magic had failed and that Elise was unharmed, the queen was beside herself with anger. Deceptively, she mentioned that she had some fine oil with which to beautify the skin, but instead she took a phial of evil paste and spread it on the maiden's limbs; she poured foul oil on Elise's face and rubbed it into her skin; lastly, she scooped up ashes from the hearth and mingled them in the princess's hair.

Later, when Elise was presented to the king her skin was

streaked and brown and she looked, indeed, a very shabby creature.

"This wretch is no daughter of mine!" said the king crossly and his words brought tears to Elise's eyes. In despair she looked around for her brothers but they were nowhere to be seen; then, sobbing bitterly, she ran from the palace.

She stumbled blindly along, far away and into the great forest. Her brothers must have been banished, she thought, and her heart was filled with sadness. Night fell and she had just one desire – to find them.

The sun was already high in the sky when at last she awoke to the soft chuckling of a nearby stream. Elise rose and followed the stream's ferny bank until it tinkled into a clear, sparkling pool. The bushes grew thickly to its edge, except where the forest creatures had trod a narrow path when they came to drink; here, Elise knelt by the cool water. So clear and still was it that every leaf and twig was reflected as in a mirror. She bent over and her own face peered back at her. She was astonished: her face looked coarse and grimy. She took up a handful of water and washed it over her brow, her fair skin shone through the vile brown streaks of oil. Standing, she took off her robe and stepped into the crystal water to bathe. When at last she was clean, she stepped from the pool. No princess ever looked as graceful, so fair and beautiful was she.

She cupped her hand and drank from the pool, then she dressed, braided her hair and set off through the forest.

She walked deeper and deeper into the trees until, at twilight, the shadows grew long and dark. It was cold and the trees closed about her like somber black sentinels. A silence settled on the forest and Elise was filled with a deep loneliness. At last, exhausted, she lay down to sleep.

Elise woke early and set off. She struggled through the tangled bushes and suddenly, she came upon an old woman who was picking wild berries. She offered her humble gatherings to Elise and when the grateful princess had eaten, she asked for news of her brothers.

The old woman was thoughtful. "No," she said at last. "I have not seen eleven princes, but eleven swans have I seen – and each with a golden crown, swimming in a stream." The old woman pointed a finger: "It is close by, I will show you if you wish."

She took Elise by the hand and quite soon they came to the edge of a steep cliff, at its foot a spring gurgled out into a twisting stream.

"Thank you, kind lady," said Elise and she clambered down the rocky cliff. She picked her way along the ferny banks searching for the swans, but at last the stream widened into a river and opened into the sea.

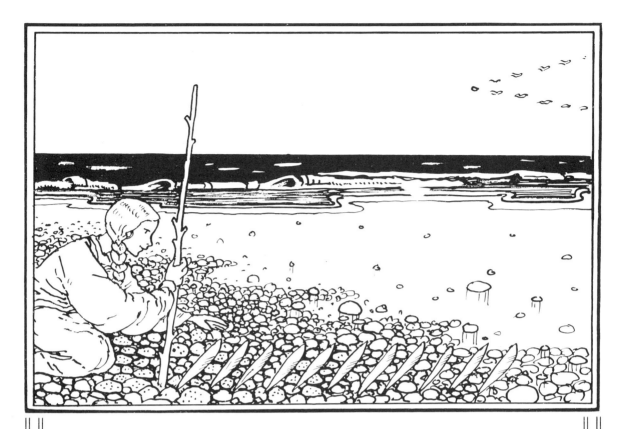

The shore was deserted: no boat, or ship, or any living being was to be seen, just the vast rolling ocean. Elise could go no farther – her journey seemed to be at an end. Despairingly, she slumped down on the pebbled beach; she thought that now she would never find her lost brothers. As she sat there, idly toying with a pebble, she became thoughtful: the pebble felt smooth and round in her hand. All about her were stones and glass, iron and flint and all washed smooth by the constant waves. The waters, softer than her own fair hand, had ground down the rocky shore turning it into the fine polished pebbles beside her.

"It is a lesson you have taught me," Elise spoke softly to the waves. "Your waters take many years but at last shape the hardest stone. I too, must be as constant, and by not tiring, find my dear lost brothers."

The seaweed crackled at her feet and looking down, Elise saw eleven swan-white feathers; each with a single pearl of dew – or perhaps it was a tear. She picked them up and though alone, she felt no longer lonely.

Elise gazed along the sparkling fan of the setting sun and saw eleven swans, threaded like a silken ribbon through the golden evening sky. They landed close by her on the shore and, with the sun's last radiant flare, they vanished: in their place stood eleven handsome princes. Elise had found her brothers!

She ran towards them calling their names. Their joy was overwhelming and they laughed and cried, and kissed and flung their arms about each other. The eldest of her brothers took her hand and told their tale.

"From dawn to dusk we fly as wild swans do – the sunset bids us land and gives us back our form as men. Should we be above the clouds when the sun goes down we would surely fall and be dashed to pieces on the ground." The other brothers nodded and drew close about her.

"Far away across the ocean there is a land of great beauty and splendor and, such is our fortune, it is there that we must now live. Despite its beauty it is not our homeland and we may return here only in the middle of the year when the days are at their longest. The ocean's span is wide and the journey tiring and there is but one small rock where we may rest: no island peeps its head above the waves, no other shelter can we find. The rock is small and we must cling together closely lest we drown. If storms blow up we suffer dismally, for the wind lashes the waves into foam and whips us cruelly. But without that lonely rock we could never fly to see our dear sweet homeland."

Elise was saddened by their story but her brother spoke again. "We can only stay for eleven days: it is enough, but barely, to cross the forest and see our home. We can look down once more on the chapel where our dear mother lies buried. It is as if we were children again: the same wild horses gallop on the plain; the same sweet songs float up to us from charcoal-burners' camps. These memories bring us back, but sadly, for so short a time.

"Now, dear sister, we have found you, but in two more days we must return across the sea. How can we take you with us?" Elise had no answer to his question. The night wore on until, just before dawn, they lay down and slept.

Elise woke to the sound of beating wings and above her she saw eleven white swans wheeling. It was her brothers once more transformed. They turned and flew high over the tree tops, but one sank down, her youngest brother, and stayed with her all day. He placed his head upon her lap and she stroked his snow-white wing. Later, the others returned and with the night, they were as men again.

"Tomorrow we must leave," said the eldest brother. "But to leave you behind us is too sad a thought to bear. As a man I could carry you lightly, so surely all our wings together could bear you up. Will you come with us, dear sister?"

"Yes, dear loves, I will come," Elise smiled and took their hands.

Through the night the princes worked, weaving a quilt of willow and reeds. When morning came the princes turned into swans again: they settled around the quilt and taking it in their beaks, they flew up into the cool morning air. Elise was so tired from the night's efforts that she slept soundly on the floating quilt. Up through the clouds they flew and into the bright sunshine. The sun was strong upon her face so the youngest swan flew above to shade her.

When at last she awoke she marveled at her magic flight, so swiftly did they travel through the air. All day the ocean rolled beneath them, but later the sky grew dark and storm clouds gathered. Her weight, though slight, had slowed them down and Elise became fearful and looked out for the lonely rock. The empty ocean spread in all directions, no rock appeared to ease her fears and she prayed to herself that her brothers' lives be spared. The sun was sinking fast and all the while their wings beat harder.

The black clouds tumbled angrily and a lashing wind howled against them. Below, the waves grew fierce and steep, and flashed from black to white-capped jade as the lightning crackled. Elise was sure they'd now all drown and she clung, trembling, to the quilt, but then the swans dived down. They plunged so swiftly that she thought the sea would swallow them, but just as the waves reached up to snatch them from the sky, the swans slowed and hovered: below them Elise could see the tiny rock. The sun fell below the broken sea in a last purple glare and as it did so they landed safely.

As men again, the brothers linked their arms around Elise, while through the night the dreadful storm raged on.

When dawn came the fury of the gale was spent but the sea still ran high and wild. Once more the swans flapped into the air, gently lifting Elise on her frail bed.

They journeyed on across the foam-whipped ocean and it was long after that Elise saw a ragged spine of mountain peaks pierce the horizon. As they drew close she saw they were thickly wooded with cedar, cypress and pine. Tiny castles and cities were dotted among the trees.

At last the swans flew down and landed. Close by was a deep cave with its walls and floor thickly carpeted with vines and creepers. When sunset came her youngest brother took her by the hand and led her to the cave. "Here you will sleep, dear sister, and in the morning you will tell us of your dreams."

Elise smiled at him: "My dream will lift the curse that binds you."

She slept and in her dreams she drifted to a high castle set among the clouds. As she looked at it a young and beautiful fairy came from the castle gate towards her.

"Is it you who will give me the secret to break the spell?" asked Elise. The fairy nodded.

"You must be brave and tireless if the spell is to be broken," said the fairy. "You have learned the lesson of the soft waters on the rocky shore. But stones, unlike your soft hand, do not feel pain. They know no fear as does your pure heart. They do not suffer as you must." The fairy bent and plucked a stinging nettle from the ground.

"Nettles like this grow around the cave in which you sleep, and others like it grow in churchyard graves: no others must you pick, only these. Let not the pain you feel deter you from your task. Scatter the nettles on the ground and crush them with your bare feet; they will burn and blister but you must not stop until you have pounded them to fiber. From the fiber you must spin thread and weave cloth, enough for eleven shirts with long sleeves. Dress each of your brothers in the shirts and the spell will be broken. But do not forget this: though it may take you years, at no time must you utter a single word. You must be silent until the work is finished. Should one word escape your lips it will drive a dagger through the hearts of your brothers. Their lives are held safe only by your silence."

The fairy leaned forward and touched the nettle to Elise's arm. Immediately a searing pain burned like fire on her skin and she woke up – beside her lay the nettle.

Elise left the cave and did as she had been told. With each nettle she picked, her hands and wrists became burned and blistered, but despite her suffering she did not falter in her work, so determined was she to free her brothers. She trampled the nettles under her bare feet and spun the fibers into fine, nettle-green thread.

When her brothers returned in the evening they were puzzled by her

silence. Then they saw her cruelly swollen hands and one of them, weeping, bent to kiss them; his tears washed her fingers and the painful blisters vanished.

For a day and two nights she did not sleep and at last the first shirt was finished. Carefully she folded it and laid it aside.

The next day as she sat spinning her thread she heard the doleful bay of hunting hounds. She quickly gathered up her nettles and thread and the one completed shirt and fled into the cave. Within seconds the great dogs crashed through the bushes and, snarling savagely, trapped her in the cave. She crouched there trembling, but then a band of huntsmen rode into the clearing.

They dismounted and one of them approached the mouth of the cave. He was truly handsome and was, in fact, the king in those parts. Elise, sitting wide-eyed on her bundle of nettles, was the fairest maiden he had ever seen.

"Why do you hide such grace as yours inside so grim a place, my child?" His voice was kind but Elise dare not answer his question. He bent and took her hand: "This is no place for you," he said. "If your heart is as pure as your image is beautiful, I will dress you in the finest robes and you will live in my grandest palace."

Elise made no protest as he lifted her onto his horse, but her heart was full of despair and she wept bitterly as they galloped away.

When they reached the palace she remained silent. Maidservants bathed her and wove tiny pearls into her hair. They dressed her in silken robes and covered her ill-used hands with golden gloves. One sight of her slender beauty as she entered the court was enough for the king; he vowed there and then to make her his queen. The archbishop, who stood at the king's elbow, however, was grim-faced. "This wood-maiden is surely a witch," he wheezed. "She has clouded Your Majesty's judgement."

The king brushed aside his protests and ordered a great celebration to

begin. There was feasting, dancing and music; Elise was shown the wonders of the palace and led through its flower-filled gardens. Yet, despite the king's attentions she remained sad and not the slightest smile touched her lips. At last, in desperation, he led her up to a small chamber high in a tower. He had made it just like her cave: tapestries hung from the walls and there, on the green-cushioned floor, he had placed her bundle of nettles and thread, and the single finished shirt.

She turned and smiled at him: now she could finish her work and release her brothers from the evil spell. The king was overjoyed by her smile: she would be his bride, he thought, and he kissed her tenderly. Soon after the wedding took place.

Time passed and she said not a word to the king. Her eyes told him of the love she felt for him, but until her work was finished, she must remain silent.

At night she would leave the king's bed, go up to her little room and spin and weave until dawn. Soon, the nettle thread was all used up: only six of the shirts were finished and she must pick more nettles to complete the remaining five.

Outside the palace wall was a churchyard and in it grew the nettles that she needed. "God will aid me," she thought, for she was fearful of discovery. "The pain in my hands will not match that in my heart."

When the night was black she crept like a thief from the castle and went to the churchyard. As she tiptoed along between the graves the moon slid out from behind a cloud. She drew in her breath; not an arm's length away were the ghouls. They sat on a grave having eaten their fill, they had the heads and the breasts of women and their snake-like bodies were twisted and twined together. They watched her pass, their sunken eyes unblinking and evil. Elise said a prayer, but her heart was pounding with fear.

Later that night the archbishop sat at his darkened window, his sore sleepless eyes gazing into the night. Only he saw her step through the gates of the castle, carrying her bundle of nettles – only he was awake. "So, I was right," he hissed. "She is a witch!"

Of course, he told the king and the king wept for love of his dear wife. He could no longer sleep and when Elise next left his bed, he followed. Night after night she worked in the green chamber, and night after night the king silently watched. His face became drawn and gray from lack of sleep and Elise, looking fondly at her husband, wondered at his mournful manner.

There was only one more shirt to make but she needed still more nettles. Elise shuddered at the thought of retracing her steps through the terrible churchyard, but that night she set off again.

The king followed her once more, but this time he was accompanied by the smug archbishop. They saw her enter the churchyard and they saw the ghouls. The king was sad beyond belief. "How could she share my bed and lie with me, yet meet such loathsome creatures in the night?" he wept. "The people shall judge her," he murmured at last.

And they did, and found her guilty – she must burn at the stake.

Elise was taken from her fine chambers and thrown into a dungeon deep in the pit of the castle. It was damp and there was no bed to lie on, but just as the jailer was closing the door, he threw in her bundle of shirts and the remaining nettles. "Here, use this rubbish for a pillow," he growled. "And take your coats for a blanket, . . . not that you deserve them." And he slammed the door shut.

Elise could have wept for joy at these unexpected gifts: there was still hope. She worked frantically all day and late in the afternoon she heard the beating of wings, it was her youngest brother. She peered through the iron grille of her window and saw him swooping by; knowing they were close gave her new strength and once more she set to work.

*　　　*　　　*

It was time! Elise was dragged from her cell and thrown into a filthy cart. Quickly she picked up the bundle of shirts and the one that was still to be finished. The crowd jeered and spat on her as she passed by, silently praying. Her lips trembled and she shivered as the cart rumbled along, and all the time her fingers sewed feverishly at the last shirt.

"See!" screamed the people. "She is still not sorry! She persists with her wicked magic! Tear it from her! Rip it to shreds!" The crowd was angry and began to pull savagely at the sides of the cart, but a great flapping noise startled them and they drew back. Eleven swans swooped down and perched around the edge of the cart; they ruffled their feathers and hissed at the throng.

The cart trundled at last into the cobbled square; in the center stood a tall stake and around its foot were piled bundles of dry brushwood. The people were eager to see the burning of the witch. The executioner reached up to drag her from the cart but Elise shrunk back, took up the pile of shirts and threw them over the backs of the eleven swans. Instantly, eleven handsome princes ringed the cart. Strong young men, save one, the youngest: he still had a white swan's wing instead of an arm. Despite her efforts Elsie had not quite managed to finish the sleeve of the last nettle shirt.

"I am innocent!" she cried. These were her first words and the crowd was stunned into silence. Then, a whisper ran through their number: goodness had prevailed over evil and one by one, they knelt and prayed. Poor Elise, so weak from lack of food and sleep and exhausted by her labors, swooned into the arms of her eldest brother.

Supporting her gently, he told the king of their misfortune and of Elise's silent ordeal. The king smiled tenderly at his bride, his heart was full of remorse and he leaned close to her. As if by a signal the air became thick with the sweetest perfume and the king paused. The brushwood by the stake was curling and twisting, turning from lifeless kindling into a green rose briar. Pure blooms opened up their petals like a hundred tiny suns; each was perfection in its beauty.

The king reached up and plucked the highest rose. He laid it softly on Elise's breast. Slowly, she opened her eyes and looked up at him; she smiled and reaching out, gently brushed his cheek with her fingertips.

That single moment touched the whole city. And, for ever after, the king and the beautiful Elise and her eleven brothers and the people of the town were happy and contented.

The Emperor's New Clothes

LONG AGO THERE LIVED AN EMPEROR who only cared about clothes. He spent each and every day dressing up in the finest robes. He was never seen in the same clothes from one hour to the next. His thoughts were on shoes not soldiers, coats not councils, tunics not taxes and gloves instead of governments. People got quite used to his ways and in their talk, instead of saying: "God's in his heaven, so all is right" they would say: "The emperor's in his wardrobe, things must be fine."

The town was large and prosperous, the townsfolk busied themselves about their trade and, all in all, they were very happy. Visitors came and went, buying and selling this and that, or just admiring the town itself. One day, however, two visitors arrived who were very different – they were cheats and tricksters.

They set up shop as weavers of fine cloth and put about their tale: they could, they said, weave a cloth of the most marvelous quality; of the most diverse variety of pattern and color. The cloth was also special in another way, it could only be seen by the cleverest, noblest, most wise and fitting of people. To those of lesser character and with stupid heads, it would remain invisible.

The word soon spread throughout the town and, as would be expected, the news soon reached the emperor. "Ah, that cloth I would dearly like to see," he thought. "And, . . ." he preened in front of his mirror. "I shall also be able to see who among my court is clever and who is stupid."

Straightaway he sent for the weavers. Money was no object: he would have some of the cloth prepared for himself without delay and he paid the weavers handsomely in advance for their services. They asked for gold and silver threads to work into the cloth, and perhaps some precious stones for decoration. Nothing was denied them, although

these items were never seen again. The weavers started work. They set up their loom and sat all day and night weaving away.

The emperor waited and waited. "When will they finish weaving my cloth?" he thought. But despite his impatience about the progress of the work, the thought of not being able to see the cloth bothered him greatly. "If I can't see it, I will be thought stupid and that will never do. I must send someone else to find out how things are going."

He summoned his prime minister, instructed him of his duties, and sent him on his way.

The prime minister did as he was bid but when he entered the weaver's shop he couldn't believe his eyes. The loom was empty!

"But, . . . where is, . . . " he stammered, but stopped himself just in time. He dare not say more lest he be thought an idiot and be thrown out of office. He blinked, rubbed his eyes and looked again. The loom was still empty; he could still not see any cloth. He was so confused he just stood there with his mouth open.

"You may well gasp," said the weavers. "Isn't it the finest cloth you have ever seen? Here, feel the fine quality. Look at the beauty of the pattern." As if he was holding a piece of cloth the weaver held out his empty hands. The minister was now so shocked that all he could do was pretend. He rubbed his thumb and finger together as if feeling the cloth. "It's the finest, the best, the most beautiful I've, . . . ever . . . seen," he mumbled. "The emperor will be delighted."

The prime minister took note of all the things the weavers had said: which pattern went where, how the color was arranged, and, of course, their demands for more money.

"Materials are so expensive, good sir," they whined. "We will surely need more gold and silver thread in order to complete the cloth."

More days passed and once again the emperor sent for news of the cloth. This time he sent a clerk to check the weaver's progress.

"Sir, I can't believe it myself, some days," the oily weavers bowed and scraped. "Is that not, without doubt, the finest piece of cloth you've ever seen?" The clerk could not see anything but he chose to remain silent. He could see the empty loom but not the cloth. Then, recovering his senses he said: "Of course, of course. Without question. It is superb!" The poor clerk left as quickly as he could, feeling very upset. "Can I really be that stupid," he asked as he hurried back to the emperor's palace.

The marvelous cloth became the talk of the town and at last the emperor set off to see it for himself. He took with him his ministers and clerks, his council and the court and his men-at-arms. "They shall see it too," he said.

The prime minister was the first to break the silence in the weaver's shop. "What do you think, Your Majesty? Isn't it superb!"

The emperor gulped. "Are my eyes deceiving me," he thought. "Where is the cloth? I can't see a single thread. Surely *I'm* not stupid – I must pretend that I can see it. No one must know that I can't, otherwise I'll be thrown off the throne." The weavers smiled and bobbed and bowed in front of the emperor.

"It's wonderful!" he said.

"And look at the fantastic colors!" added the clerk. The rest of the

gathering crowded forward: they could see nothing but each believed that all around him could. "Oh yes! Such pattern! What texture! What fine quality!" They heaped their praises on the unseen cloth. The emperor, they said, must surely order a suit of robes for the coming town procession. They left, but not before the weavers had again been rewarded for their labors.

As the day of the procession drew near the light in the weaver's shop burned long into the night. The townsfolk peered through the windows and were amazed. There sat an empty loom, yet the weavers wound invisible cloth from it; they carried invisible cloth to their cutting table; they flashed their scissors through the air and then sat, cross-legged, sewing at nothing.

At last the word came that the clothes were finished. Down came the clerks, and the court and the council, and the men-at-arms – at their head strode the emperor.

The weavers stood with hands behind backs. "What do you think, Your Majesty," they chorused. They took hold of the air and held up the air and showed the air to the emperor. "Notice the detail on the shirt and trousers," they chirped. "See the trim of the coat and the fall of the train. Isn't it just what His Majesty had hoped for?"

The emperor gulped but all around him his courtiers mumbled their approval.

"Now, if Your Majesty will remove the, er, . . . fine suit he is wearing at present, we will re-attire him."

His imperial pink majesty stood before the long mirror. The weavers lifted his arms and slipped on a shirt he could not see. He stepped into trousers he could not see and raised his chin while a cloak he could not see was buckled under his throat.

"Oh, what a perfect fit! And so suited to Your Majesty's fine bearing." The courtiers clasped their hands together and leaned back in admiration. None would dare declare that, as far as they could see, the emperor wore nothing. Nothing at all!

The great procession started. Leading the way, striding out quite proudly, was the emperor. Indeed, his clothes were as light as a feather, he could not even feel them. Behind him came two footmen holding their finger tips together in the air. They looked a little worried; each pretending to carry the emperor's train but neither of them would dare to say that he could neither see nor feel it.

Through the town they went, and people lined the streets and cheered. None there could see the emperor's clothes, yet none would dare speak of it for fear of being thought stupid.

"Bravo!" they called. "What splendid clothes! What style! What taste! How well his Majesty looks! Such finery!"

But then a small voice was heard among the crowd. "But he has nothing on!" It was a child.

The people close to the child hushed him, but thought: "The child is right! He has nothing on!" The words spread throughout the crowd.

"But he has nothing on!"

The poor emperor trudged on. "How stupid have I been. They are right," he thought. "I do have nothing on!"